...ver Forget You

A very long, long, long time ago,
a little Spinosaurus went to the
seashore to pick red berries.

Just then . . .

TATSUYA MIYANISHI
MUSEYON, New York

ROARRR!

A Tyrannosaurus approached
with its mouth wide open
and its eyes glaring.

"Ahhh! Help!"

The little Spinosaurus hid
behind a tree, his body
trembling.

"Tough luck for you to meet me in a place like this," said the Tyrannosaurus, and . . .

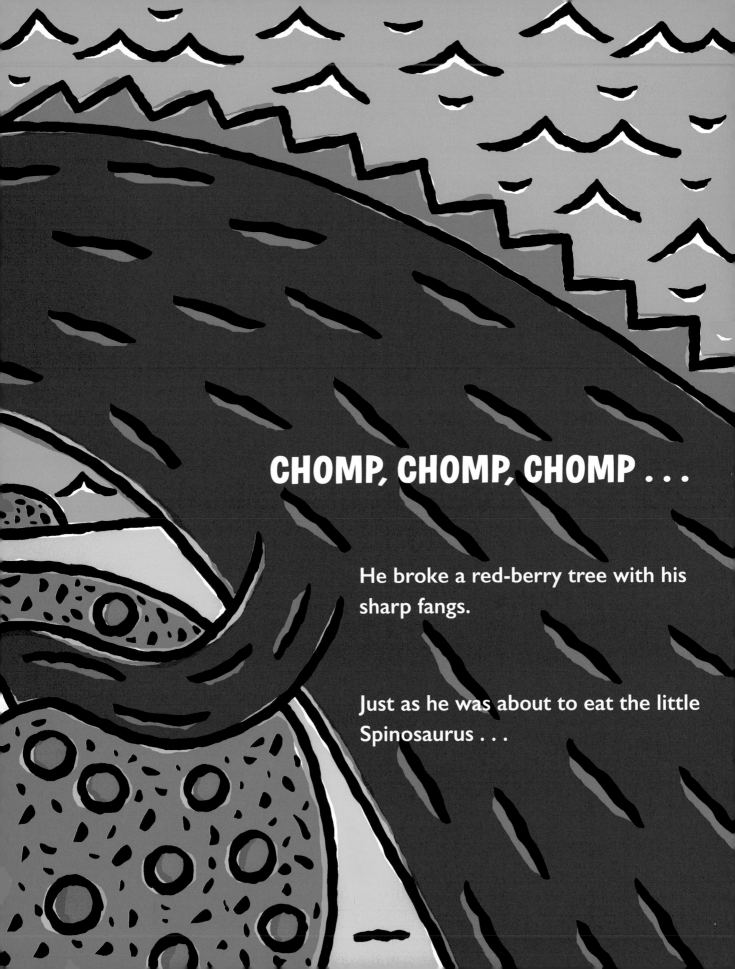

CHOMP, CHOMP, CHOMP . . .

He broke a red-berry tree with his sharp fangs.

Just as he was about to eat the little Spinosaurus . . .

RUMBLE, RUMBLE, RUMBLE . . .

A huge earthquake shook the ground.

RUMBLE, RUMBLE . . .
CRACK, CRACK . . .
The earth trembled and started to split. . . .

RUMBLE . . .

Finally the ground split completely, and the
spot where the Tyrannosaurus and the little
Spinosaurus were standing floated away.

RUMBLE . . .

"I-I . . .
can't swim,"
whimpered the Tyrannosaurus.

"I-I can't swim, either. . . .
What . . . will happen to us now?"
The little Spinosaurus started to cry.

"What do you mean by 'What will happen to us now?' I'm going to eat you!" The Tyrannosaurus snatched up the little Spinosaurus. . . .

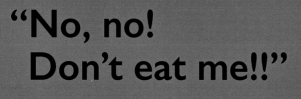

"No, no!
Don't eat me!!"

shouted the little
Spinosaurus.

He spoke fast.
"I-I am so good at catching
fish, you know.
I'll catch lots of lots of fish for
you starting today, Mister.
You can eat fish. Every day.
Fish and more fish.
You can eat all the tasty fish
you want.

But if you eat me now, you will be hungry
all the time from tomorrow, you know.
You don't want that, do you?
That's why—that's why you can't eat me!
You do understand that? You understand it?
Right?"

"Can you really catch fish?"
The Tyrannosaurus put the Spinosaurus down.
Instantly the little Spinosaurus dunked his
face into the ocean and . . . came right back
up with a fish in his mouth.

The Tyrannosaurus was delighted.
"Munch, munch, munch. Yum, yum, yum. Bring back more!"
Since the Tyrannosaurus ate a lot of fish, the little
Spinosaurus got tired of catching fish.

That's how they started living together,
alone on the tiny island.

One evening . . .

"My name is Wimpy," said the Spinosaurus.
"Everyone calls me that because I'm a crybaby.
What is your name, Mister?"

"M . . . my name is . . . I don't have one."

"So, your name is I Don't Have One, isn't it?"
"Whatever," said the Tyrannosaurus.

"Uh, Mister I Don't Have One,
what brought you here?"

"The day the earthquake happened,
I was here because I thought I could find
something delicious to eat. What about
you? Why did you come here?"

Wimpy answered in a sad voice.
"My mom is sick.
Mister Pteranodon told me that these
red berries could heal her. . . ."

"Oh. So, you came here for your mom,"
said the Tyrannosaurus.

Wimpy started to cry.
"I wonder if my mom is okay.
Is she waiting for me to come back?"

"Listen, Wimpy, your mom should be okay. She'll be waiting for your return," the Tyrannosaurus told Wimpy gently.

"Th-thank you, Mister."

No one had ever said "THANK YOU" to the Tyrannosaurus before.

The next day, as Wimpy was going to catch fish,
the Tyrannosaurus smiled and said,
"Let's eat red berries today instead of fish."
The Tyrannosaurus gathered plenty of red berries,
and Wimpy was overjoyed.
"You are amazing, Mister!"

No one had ever called the Tyrannosaurus
AMAZING before.

"Try some, Mister," Wimpy said.
The Tyrannosaurus gulped a bunch of berries.
"Yum! These may be even more delicious than you.
HEH, HEH, HEH!"

"Told you so, hee, hee, hee. You are so funny, Mister."
No one had ever called the Tyrannosaurus FUNNY before.

Watching Wimpy eat, the Tyrannosaurus thought,
I wish his mom could eat some red berries.

The next day, suddenly out of the sky, a Tapejara flew down and tried to snatch Wimpy.

One night
Wimpy thought of his mom
and began to sob.

The Tyrannosaurus didn't say a
word but hugged him tight.

Wimpy wiped his tears and said,
"You are very kind, Mister."

No one had ever called the
Tyrannosaurus KIND before either.

Every time Wimpy said,
"THANK YOU," "You're
AMAZING," "You're
FUNNY," "You're COOL,"
or "You're KIND," the
Tyrannosaurus felt his
heart get warmer.

He started to tell Wimpy,
"I'm so—"
Just then . . .

RUMBLE, RUMBLE, RUMBLE . . .

Another big earthquake!

RUMBLE, RUMBLE . . .
CRACK, CRACK . . .
The earth trembled, and the little
island began moving.

To their surprise, they were moving toward the land they had been separated from.

They moved closer and closer. When they were almost there, the earth stopped trembling, and the island stopped moving.

"Now!"

Holding Wimpy to his chest,
the Tyrannosaurus leaped as far as he could.

The waves sparkled under them.

SPLASH!

The Tyrannosaurus fell into the water.

The red-berry tree flew out of his arms
and landed on the edge of the cliff.
"You . . . you shouldn't forget this . . .
Hu-hurry and go see your mom. . . ."

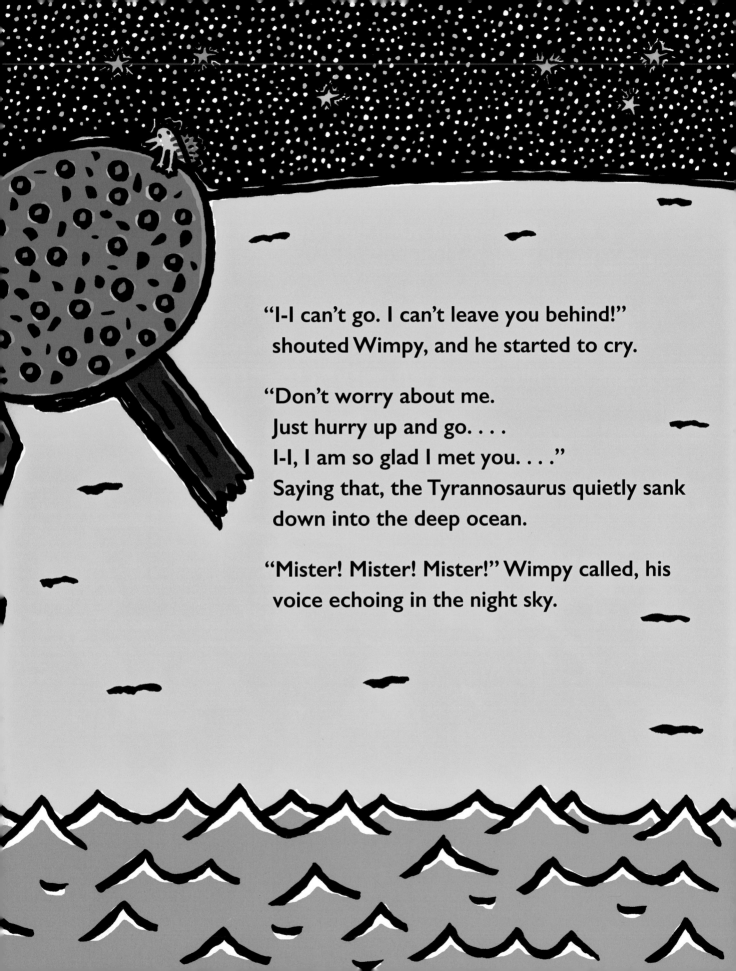

"I-I can't go. I can't leave you behind!"
shouted Wimpy, and he started to cry.

"Don't worry about me.
Just hurry up and go. . . .
I-I, I am so glad I met you. . . ."
Saying that, the Tyrannosaurus quietly sank
down into the deep ocean.

"Mister! Mister! Mister!" Wimpy called, his
voice echoing in the night sky.

Years passed, and Wimpy learned to swim.
He went back to the island and found two red berries growing
from the tree that the Tyrannosaurus had broken off.

Eating one of the berries, Wimpy imitated the Tyrannosaurus.
"Yum! This may be even more delicious than you.
HEH, HEH, HEH!"

Tears welled up in Wimpy's eyes.
"He was funny and cool, and he was truly kind. . . .
Thank you, Mister . . . **I WILL NEVER FORGET YOU.**"

About Author

Born in 1956, **Tatsuya Miyanishi** graduated from the Nihon University College of Art and was a doll artist and graphic designer before becoming a picture-book author. Miyanishi has a passionate fan base of all ages who enjoy his range of endearing characters in many genres, from superheroes to dinosaurs. The books in his Tyrannosaurus series have sold more than fifteen million copies and have been translated into many languages.

I WILL NEVER FORGET YOU

Deaete Honto ni Yokatta © 2009 Tatsuya Miyanishi
All rights reserved.

Publisher's Cataloging-in-Publication Data
Names: Miyanishi, Tatsuya, 1956- author, illustrator. | Gharbi, Mariko Shii, translator. | Kaplan, Simone, editor.
Title: I will never forget you / Tatsuya Miyanishi ; Mariko Shii Gharbi, translator ; Simone Kaplan, editor.
Other titles: Deaete hontō ni yokatta. English
Description: New York : Museyon, [2020] | Series: Tyrannosaurus series | "Originally published in Japan in 2009 by POPLAR Publishing Co., Ltd."--Title page verso. | Audience: Ages 5-7. |
Identifiers: ISBN: 9781940842448 | LCCN: 2020934662
Subjects: LCSH: Tyrannosaurus rex--Juvenile fiction. | Spinosaurus--Juvenile fiction. | Dinosaurs--Juvenile fiction. | Friendship--Juvenile fiction. | Love--Juvenile fiction. | Helping behavior--Juvenile fiction. | Caring--Juvenile fiction. | Mothers--Juvenile fiction. | Happiness--Juvenile fiction. | Self-sacrifice--Juvenile fiction. | Intercultural communication--Juvenile fiction. | CYAC: Tyrannosaurus rex--Fiction. | Spinosaurus--Fiction. | Dinosaurs--Fiction. | Friendship--Fiction. | Love--Fiction. | Helpfulness--Fiction. | Caring--Fiction. | Mothers--Fiction. | Happiness--Fiction. | Self-sacrifice--Fiction. | Communication--Fiction. | BISAC: JUVENILE FICTION / Animals / Dinosaurs & Prehistoric Creatures.
Classification: LCC: PZ7.M699575 I186 2020 | DDC: [E]--dc23

Published in the United States and Canada by:
Museyon Inc.
333 East 45th Street
New York, NY 10017

Museyon is a registered trademark.
Visit us online at www.museyon.com

Originally published in Japan in 2009 by POPLAR Publishing Co., Ltd.
English translation rights arranged with POPLAR Publishing Co., Ltd.

Printed in China

ISBN 9781940842448

I will never forget you.